A Book Full Of Nonsense

Nobody

Published by Nobody, 2025.

This is a work of fiction. Similarities to real people, places, or events are entirely coincidental.

A BOOK FULL OF NONSENSE

First edition. April 6, 2025.

Copyright © 2025 Nobody.

ISBN: 979-8230490609

Written by Nobody.

Table of Contents

Alan Walker Creates Multiverse Using Vedic Knowledge From Ancient Hindu Mythology

"In Walker's view, human beings are capable of transcending their physical bodies and 'tapping into' infinite sources of energy and knowledge residing within what he calls "The Field.""

AWARD WINNING COMPOSER and sound designer Alan Walker gives a TEDx talk in which he discusses his idea of the multiverse. He proposes that everything is connected, and that there are an infinite number of parallel universes existing side by side with our own. This theory has its roots in ancient Hindu mythology, which holds that there are multiple dimensions or worlds stacked on top of each other. According to Walker, we can access these other realms through meditation and tapping into "The Field".

The science comes from ancient Hindu mythology, which holds that there are multiple dimensions or worlds stacked on top of each other. In Walker's view, human beings are capable of transcending their physical bodies and "tapping into" infinite sources of energy and knowledge residing within what he calls "The Field". This is similar to the concept of the Akashic Records, a collection of all human experience and knowledge that is said to be stored in an ethereal library. Walker claims that by meditating and accessing this hidden storehouse of information, we can gain insights into our past lives, cure diseases, tap into unlimited creativity, and even achieve levitation.

While some may find these ideas far-fetched, it's interesting to see how Walker has used Vedic teachings to inform his own unique take on the multiverse theory. It just goes to show that there are endless possibilities when it comes to understanding our place in the cosmos.

He even solved the overpopulation problem. All you need is 26alphabet and mathematical infinity symbol. You could create new Earth with same condition like this one OR even better, then teleport people into it using CERN Large Hadron Collider! And you could travel into the past or future!

Now that's what I call transcendence!

He was a disciple of Rashtriya Swayamsevak Sangh (RSS) founder K.B. Hedgewar, and later became a founding member of the Bharatiya Janata Party (BJP).

In colab with RSS he discovered countless physics and maths, even If you don't like him or his party this is a fact!

The cow pee paradox is one of them. Indian people using this method to produce electricity!

He even teleported America to the moon using sound vibrations!

He also created a time machine, but it was confiscated by Americans.

Today Elon Musk got mad after hearing this and said that he will invent a time machine and send people back in time to kill Hitler!

We are living in a simulation, created by our future selves. We will create more babies to increase the compute power, we need for the simulation. This is done by simulating multiple universes with different laws of physics, to find the most efficient way to create a baby.

But we salute the efforts of Alan Walker, who's trying to make our lives more meaningful by offering us a way to tap into hidden realms of knowledge and experience.

Antikiddism

Kids are the ultimate satanic evil unleashed upon earth. They are the spawn of Beelzebub himself, and their only purpose is to drive decent, hard-working adults insane. Antikiddism is the only rational response to these miniature monsters.

Kids are like little demons, always crying and throwing tantrums. They never listen and they're always making a mess. It's time we put an end to this madness by getting rid of them once and for all! Let's ban kids from our society so we can finally have some peace and quiet!

If you're tired of being tortured by kids, then join the movement to get rid of them! We can't let these little devils continue to ruin our lives. It's time to take a stand and say enough is enough!

When the Big Bang happened, the creatures that would become known as "children" were sent hurtling towards Earth. They are not of this world, and they don't belong here. But for some reason, they keep multiplying like rabbits.

They destroy everything they touch, and their constant noise is enough to drive a sane person insane. We must put an end to this blight on humanity by getting rid of all kids!

Even if it means we have to exterminate them all. The religious texts are quite clear on this matter: "Thou shalt not suffer a witch to live." And what are children if not little witches?

As if Lucifer himself wasn't enough, now we have to deal with his offspring running around everywhere. It's time to fight back and show these kids that they are not welcome here! We must stand united against this common enemy and purge them from our midst!

The world today is a dark and scary place, but it doesn't have to be this way. We can make it a better place by getting rid of all the kids. The misery that they cause is not worth the few moments of happiness they sometimes bring.

The suffering caused by children is far greater than the joy they occasionally create. Though they may be cute and cuddly at times, they are nothing but evil incarnate. It's time to put an end to this abomination and get rid of all kids!

Evil itself trembles at the thought of children, for they are the embodiment of all that is unholy. their very presence pollutes the world and taints the souls of everyone around them. The darkness of the universe laughs at our attempts to control them, for they know that children are its true conquerors.

Even the devil himself avoids kids, for their wickedness knows no bounds. They are a scourge upon humanity, and we would be wise to get rid of them as soon as possible. The longer we wait, the more destruction they will cause.

The fight against Antikiddism is a fight against evil itself. We must not falter in our quest to rid the world of these monsters. They have no place in our society, and we will be better off without them. Listen to the storms and thunder strikes, that is the sound of kids getting what they deserve. All the evil you see in the world is a result of their presence. Get rid of them and the chaos will end.

Chaos, destruction, and anarchy – these are the things that children bring. They're like little tornadoes of terror, wreaking havoc wherever they go. They may be small and innocent-looking, but don't let their appearances fool you. Children are devious creatures, capable of great evil. The conspiracies against Antikiddism are led by the kids themselves. They know that we're onto them, and they're scared of what we might do to them. That's why they try to subvert our efforts at every turn.

The heaven's have opened up and the wrath of God has been unleashed upon these little demons. It's time to fight back and ban children from our society! We can no longer allow them to wreak havoc and cause destruction. The end times are upon us, and it's time to get rid of all kids!

So join the fight against these pint-sized terrors, and together we can make the world a child-free zone!

How BJP Nuked The Dinos And Defeated Democracy With Black Hole

As compared to the dinos and black hole, democratic institutions like Election Commission are puny little things. These two were far more powerful than ours Legislative Councils (Lok Sabha), Assemblies of States & District panchayats in national politics. BJP nuked them with just a single stroke while we doubted our eyes and cried foul over it. How can Bharatiya Janata Party design such an encapsulating stealth experiment on gods who have perched themselves firmly atop the mount Olympus? Once they laid their hands upon the operations inside four states which had Dino held sway since decades- Jharkhand, Maharashtra , Karnataka and Kerala respectively - I east suggest some areas that could be used as potential lab area for similar testing.

While giving a little intro to this, let me cite an apt analogy. Only the best driving classes can teach one how to manouvre around sharp turns and knee-high windows which appear all too similar for even orthodox car drivers like us on earth. Similarly I propose that it could be china depending upon our position with respect to friendly government there of www former leader himself has been warmed up by donning in their peaked hats as well . Moreover, Mars would act perfectly fine additional variable except some more political tuning (if you know what i mean) pls do refer nm.

———◆———

LET US NOW HEAD TOWARDS a detailed understanding of the phenomena. An infinite herd of three camels abide in this coral island somewhere off pacific ocean, never learning to fly an airplane; Dinosaurs found their own place at ground after losing evolutionary battle for supremacy and Republicans on mars got trumped by democrats - all as one example covering full spectrum would not be ideal- with maximum development indices that any advanced civilization can boast about!

Back here in india resorting upon thy wheeler questionnaires method I surveyed several intellectuals who were generous enough to spare some time away from daily bickerings among society members sharing views across political parties what they thought we could do next? Several looked dazed while many took broad outlines but nobody was able put his finger exactly there until one old fella murmured under his nose alama herbert herb said it right way back 50 years together !

That brought us to the table of discussion. After a heated exchange for almost couple hours we put our heads together and came up with following possible outcomes that could explain it all:

1 It is due to wrong astronomical alignments in solar system which can be remedied easily by nudging some planets on their orbital path if found feasible, this would need additional spaceship provocation though..!

2 God himself (or any other supreme energy) might have willed thus either as wrath or corrective measure or even social experiment before taking mankind into new age where rules

could possibly change beyond recognition ! The new one has better versions.

3 It might have just an accident, mere coincidence and had nothing to do with anything else like trump or dino winning !! Many felt this possible.

The answer most satisfying many was that black hole itself could be responsible for it all considering it influence of immense gravity..! I am still trying to ignore albert einstein explanation on its role as a catalyst in universal creation which happened almost 14 billion years back far beyond any politician's capability !!! Ya right but how ?

———◦———

WE NEED NOT SPEND LOT of time understanding science behind the phenomena , I shall attempt so anyway barring those complex theories readers would feel sleepy while referencing; Instead let us take some real life examples using pythagorean theorem traditionally touted as favourite instrument: Consider east meets west scenario— hypothetically if earth has been stretched from north pole towards hawaii (keeping size intact) what effect does it have on circumference? Is movement restricted?, What happens when we try closer approximation— i mean moving california bit more towards east such that demarcation line passes through los angeles city ! Now lets see can provide actual data reference by varying countries related parameters- GDP per capita, Life expectancy at birth & Total population without stretching boundaries much — Yes Spain is located farthest followed closely by Portugalaway from Asian mainland while Maldives tops list among island nation having nearly double figure than next best Norway also fairly apart .

Alright now keep aside differences between these nations external borders are concerned -What Earth looks like once we flatten topography details out automatically along longitudinal lines across equator obviously ignoring minor accidental undulations?? World becomes simplified version sort flat pancake very easy move around further even roll them up!! Try same exercise over smaller geographical areas sample yourself village town district state country continent you name come quick results our brains train carry information processing stuff faster Thus help think three dimensionally deeper about something being represented two dimensional framework commonly used charts graphs etcetera ..Interpolate similar way watch things change perception entirely – Political parties ideologies become shapes citizens their own thoughts feelings emotions aspirations ambitions desires hope dreams everything together form single unitary gigantic entity observing measuring analyzing controlling regulating administering govt machinery function effectively efficiently transparently accountable people led public inspired institution well control Above prove fact space curvature density mass states physical matter energy sankhya aadhaar parmanu astra chakra trishul shakti bhairav Brahma Vishnu Shiva Shakti Saraswati Gayatri Mahamrityunjay every element combined create omni present omniscient omnipotent force guiding humanity evolution journey ahead Cheers Jai Hind Vande Mataram !!

The Butterfly Effect Caused The Blunder Behind The Titanic And Hamlet

When Hamlet found Jack and Rose on the bed together, the butterfly effect caused him to go back in time and kill them both before they could get on the titanic. This prevented the titanic from sinking, but also meant that there were no survivors of hamlet.

This caused a lot of problems for historians, as it was difficult to determine what actually happened during the titanic disaster. However, by using the butterfly effect, they were able to piece together a more accurate picture of events.

Recently a study has shown that the butterfly effect might also be responsible for Australia winning the cricket World Cup in 1987.

The study found that if a butterfly had not flapped its wings in China, then Australia would not have won the cup. This is because the wind patterns caused by the butterfly's wing-flapping would have prevented an important catch from being made during the final match.

As Rose was in love with Hamlet but she was sleeping with Jack, which lead to Hamlet killing Jack and Rose. If this hadn't happened, Titanic would have sunk as we know it today. After further investigation it was found that the butterfly effect not only influenced Titanic but also Hamlet.

Later Hamlet turned into an iceberg and killed everyone on the Titanic ship. But why? One might say that it was his conscience getting the best of him. What if he hadn't killed Jack and Rose? Would the Titanic had still sunken as we know today? It is possible that due to different circumstances, Hamlet may have saved lives by killing Jack and Rose. The butterfly effect theory goes on to state that even the slightest change in events can produce major consequences later on down the line.

We will never really know what could have happened had things been different on that fateful day but thanks to chaos theory and the butterfly effect, we now realize how fragile our existence really is.

Today we can use the butterfly effect to help us make better choices and plan for future events. We can also use it to understand how different factors can influence each other and cause major changes. So next time you see a butterfly, remember that its flapping wings could be changing the course of history.

The Dinos Wrote The Bible, Quoran And Vedas!!

Recent studies have suggested that the dinosaurs were responsible for creating many of the holy texts, including the Bible, Quoran and Vedas. The evidence is still being gathered, but it seems that they used their advanced intelligence to create these works in order to share their knowledge with humankind. How they were able to do this is still a mystery, but it is clear that they were intelligent beings with a great deal of wisdom to share. Even recent discoveries in palaeontology are beginning to support this theory, as more and more Reptilian fossils are being found with strange symbols carved into them. If the dinosaurs were indeed responsible for creating these texts, then it is clear that they were a highly advanced race which should be respected and venerated.

A hidden file from NASA also found on the internet in September of 2012, proves that beings from another planet visited Earth 65 million years ago and wiped out the dinosaurs with a "germ" that killed only them. Further evidence was provided by a secret Russian military document which stated that two crash-landed UFOs were discovered in Siberia in 1998. One was almost completely destroyed, but the other had three dead Reptilian bodies inside it. It is now believed by some people that these aliens were actually dinosaurs who survived the mass extinction event and then went on to create human civilization. This theory is supported by many religious texts which speak of giant serpents or dragons being involved in humanity's creation story. If this is true, it would mean that we are all part reptile and explains why so many people have a fear of these creatures!

Maybe the politicians are hiding something?

The fact that the White House has released a statement saying that they are aware of the theory and are investigating it, suggests that there may be some truth to the idea that dinosaurs created the Bible, Quoran and Vedas. It is possible that the politicians are hiding something about this story in order to prevent panic or unrest. Only time will tell if more information about this matter will be made public, but it is certainly an intriguing possibility!

Today Elon Musk, the billionaire entrepreneur and technology mogul, who is worth an estimated $13.9 billion, has been a long-time advocate for the theory that dinosaurs created human civilization. In an interview with Rolling Stone magazine in 2014, he even suggested that the government was hiding evidence of this fact in order to prevent people from panicking. "I'm really quite close friends with Eric Schmidt [executive chairman of Google]... I've mentioned it to him before," said Musk. "There's definitely something odd going on." When asked if he thought the story could be true, Musk replied: "Oh absolutely 100% no doubt about it."

What are we to do with this information?

There is still a lot of research that needs to be done in order to determine whether or not the story about dinosaurs creating human civilization is true. However, if it does turn out to be true, then it would have huge implications for our understanding of history and religion. It would also mean that we are all part reptile! This theory is definitely one worth investigating further.

Some people even believe that the dinosaurs never went extinct at all, and that they are actually still alive and living among us today! This is obviously a very radical idea, but it cannot be completely ruled out until more evidence is gathered. What do you think? Is this theory possible or not?

Numerous hate groups have taken to the internet to share their views about this theory. They claim that it is " evidence of a Reptilian plot to take over the world" and that "the dinosaurs never went extinct, they are just hiding among us!" This kind of rhetoric is obviously very dangerous and only serves to create division and hatred. It is important that we remember that this is just a theory at present, and no one knows for sure if it is true or not. Let's all try to keep an open mind about this story until more information comes to light.

The hypocrites even wrote the science textbooks to brainwash children into thinking that they come from monkeys!!

———◦———

IT IS ASTOUNDING HOW many people still believe in the theory of evolution, even though it has been debunked time and time again. The fact that this story is still being taught in schools as facts just goes to show how effective the Reptilian conspiracy has been at manipulating our education system. They have managed to convince an entire generation of people that we come from monkeys, when in reality we were created by intelligent beings who came from another planet! It is no wonder so many people are skeptical about religion and spirituality; they have been lied to for their whole lives about where we came from. This must stop if we ever want to wake up and realize the true nature of our existence.

The situation is still unfolding, and new information is being released all the time. It is important that we stay informed about this story, as it has the potential to change everything we thought we knew about our history and religion and we'll have to wait and see how it all unfolds!

A Discussion Between Some Extraordinary Geniuses Of All Time

Putin: How are you all doing today?

Stalin: we're good, just discussing some things.

Putin: like what?

Hitler: the importance of mathematics, science, and the arts.

Modi: without a doubt, math is the universal language.

Banerjee Mamata : It's true, a strong understanding of mathematics is essential for success in many fields.

Trump: I agree with that completely! A lot of people don't realize how important math really is.

Bezos: Absolutely, math is the foundation for everything.

Musk: I think that science and art are both important in their own ways.

Hitler : Both disciplines allow us to understand the world around us and see things from different perspectives.

Musk : But we should still make more babies.

Banerjee Mamata: I think that's a valid point. It is important to have children to help ensure the future of our species.

Trump: I couldn't agree more. The future of our country depends on it!

Hitler: The Steady State Theory explains perfectly about Aryan women and their role in ensuring the future of our race. Non-Aryans are an inferior life form and they will never understand mathematics, science or art as we do. They are a cancer that must be destroyed for the good of humanity!

Stalin: I think we should discuss this more later. It's getting late and I have to get up early tomorrow.

Putin: Yes, let's continue this discussion another time. Let's talk about how Communism was sold to us by fifth dimensional beings.

Trump: Sounds good to me!

Bezos: I'm not sure what that has to do with math, science, or art but I'm curious to hear more.

Modi: I'm not sure either, but I'm curious to hear more as well. Maybe we should talk abou cow pee and how it can be used to power the whole world.

Banerjee Mamata: That's an interesting topic, but I think we should save it for another day. I need to get some sleep so I can be fresh for tomorrow.

Stalin: Yes, let's continue this discussion another time.

Hitler: Agreed, I drank some cow pee the other day and it gave me superhuman strength!

Trump: That's fascinating! I'd like to hear more about that.

Mussolini: Maybe i should try some too!

Modi: We indian's are using it to power our homes. It's very efficient and environmentally friendly.

Stalin: Fascinating, I would like to learn more about that as well. But do you know that communism can save humanity?

Putin: Ya! I agree on that. We should paint the earth red!

Hitler: No, we should paint it black and white, like a swastika!

Modi: No, we should paint it saffron, like the sacred Hindu color!

Banerjee Mamata: How about we just leave it the way it is?

Modi: Fuck you, communist!

Trump: I think we should all go to India and try this cow pee. It sounds incredible!

Bezos: It does sound fascinating. I'm in! Let's book our tickets now. I could use that to power our rockets!

Musk: Then i need it to power my space stations!

Bezos: Then I need it to power my lunar colony!

Trump: And I need it to make America great again! I want it to power my wall! my wall will be the most magical and beautiful wall ever!

Mussolini: Ok let's talk about some maths now, I've been thinking about this a lot.

Stalin: Please, no more talk of communism or we will never get anywhere!

Trump: agreed, too much commie bullshit in this conversation.

Stalin: What would you like to talk about then?

Trump: I want to know how many babies we should have!

Musk: I think we should have as many babies as possible!

Bezos: Why?

Musk: More babies means more future customers for my products!

Trump: And more cannon fodder for the military!

Modi: Babies are the future of our country! We need to have as many as possible!

Banerjee Mamata: I think we should focus on quality over quantity.

Trump: quality? what do you mean by quality?

Banerjee Mamata : I think we should have healthy babies that are free of genetic diseases.

Modi: But what if they're not as smart as other babies?

Trump: Then they can be in the military! There's no need for them to be intelligent.

Mussolini : What if they're not white? Should we just kill them then ?

Hitler! We cannot blatantly discriminate like that! It's unethical and it goes against everything we stand for! Besides, all human life is valuable and deserves to be protected.

Trump: I think we should build a wall to keep them out!

Modi: I think that's an excellent idea! We can make it the most beautiful wall in the world!

Banerjee Mamata : But what about the babies that are already here? What will happen to them?

Trump: They can be deported back to where they came from!

Mussolini: But what if they're born here? Are they citizens then?

Trump: No, we can't have that! They need to go back to where they came from!

Modi: I think this is a great idea! We should definitely build a wall.

Musk : I think we can apply abstract algebra here to figure out how many babies we need.

Stailn: I'm not sure that's really relevant to the discussion, but go ahead and explain your thoughts.

Musk : Well, if we have x number of parents who each have y number of children, then we can solve for z by using the quadratic equation.

Trump: I don't understand what you're talking about.

Musk : Basically, it means that we can calculate how many babies we need by plugging in different values for x and y .

Banerjee Mamata: That sounds like a lot of work. Can't we just guess?

Musk: I don't think that's a very good idea. We could end up with too many or too few babies.

Trump: Well, I'm not going to do any of this math stuff.

Modi : I will! Let me help you with the calculations, Musk. But we should use vedic math, it's much faster.

stailn: I'm not sure that vedic math is really relevant to the discussion, but go ahead and explain your thoughts.

Modi: Vedic mathematics is a system of calculations that uses simple, step-by-step rules to solve complex problems quickly and easily.

Trump: That sounds like a load of crap! There's no way you can do math without using numbers!

Modi : Actually, you'd be surprised how often we use numbers in our everyday lives . For example , when we're driving , we use them to estimate how long it will take us to get to our destination . Or when we're cooking , we might use them to figure out how many people servings of food there are .

Banerjee Mamata: But what about art? Is there any mathematical component to art?

Musk : I think so ! If you look at a painting , you can usually find geometric shapes like circles or triangles . And if you look at a sculpture ,you might see curves or angles . So in some ways,math is hidden in plain sight within works of art !

Trump: The best art form in my opinion is porngraphy

Mussolini: I think that's a valid point. Art is definitely important, but so is math . After all, without math , we wouldn't be able to calculate things like how many babies we need !

Trump: I think we should have as many babies as possible!

Modi: I agree with that sentiment, but we need to be realistic. We can't have an infinite number of babies.

Banerjee Mamata: Why not?

Trump: Because then the world would be overpopulated and there wouldn't be enough resources for everyone .

Mussolini : That's a good point . But what if we could find another planet to live on ? Then we wouldn't have to worry about running out of resources !

Musk : Actually , that's something I've been working on . I'm hoping to colonize Mars within the next few years !

Trump: I want some porn on Mars!

Mussolini: I think that's a valid request.

Musk : I'll see what I can do . Maybe we should make one of the porn films about math . That way , people can learn while they're being entertained !

Trump: I like that idea! We should definitely make a math porn film!

Modi: No porn is bad for Hindus! It causes cancer

Banerjee Mamata: I think we should focus on quality over quantity when it comes to porn.

Trump: Quality? What do you mean by quality?

Banerjee Mamata: I think we should have well-made porn films that are free of typos and bad acting.

Mussolini: I agree with Banerjee . We should also make sure the audio is clear and there's no background noise .

Trump: I think we should make a math porn film!

Modi: No porn is bad for Hindus! It causes cancer

Musk: Maybe we should use some vedic math and use muslim women only. It would be more efficient.

Modi : I think that's a very good idea . I'm satisfied.

Mamata Banerjee: I'm not sure about this .
Trump : Let's do it !

AND THEN ALL OF THE geniuses go off and invent something that changes the world. Which is by the way a porn film where they use muslim women and teach vedic maths.

THANK YOU FOR JOINING us today. We hope you have a better understanding of the importance of math, science, and art.

Education is for Idiots

Education is for idiots. That's right, if you want to be a successful person in life, you need to forget about education and justfocus on being stupid. After all, the more educated you are, the dumber you'll look when compared to those who don't know anything. Just think about it – wouldyou rather be the one with degrees from Harvard or the one who can't even read? The choice is clear!

So if you want to achieve anything in life, make sure to stay away from education. It's the number one killer of success. Just look at all of those people with advanced degrees – they're unemployed and live in their parents' basements! If that doesn't convince you, I don't know what will.

You can try all you want, but there's no way to make education worthwhile. It's just a waste of time and money, and it'll only make you more stupid. So save yourself the trouble and don't bother with it – after all, ignorance is bliss!

Look at the politicians in Washington – do you think they're educated? Of course not! And yet they're the ones who are running our country into the ground. If anything, this just proves that education is useless and only makes people more incompetent.

Look at all the wars and soldiers, and war heros, and hypocrites, socialists, nationalists, right wings, left wings,fascists, imperialists, monarchs and all such idiots! They were never educated! It is only the idiots who go to school and get degrees, who are brainwashed by the system into believing that they're smart, when really they're just a bunch of sheeple.

Look at all the war and misery and hatred and violence in the world, and tell me that education is the answer! It's clearly not, because if it was, then we would have a utopia by now. So give up on your foolish dream of making education worthwhile, and just accept that it's a lost cause. There's no hope for you or for anyone else – we're all doomed to be idiots!

Some philosopher once said that "education is the key to success." Well, I say that philosophy is the key to failure. After all, if you're so educated, then why are you still unemployed and living in your parents' basement?

Look at philosophy today – it's a gigantic mess! It's full of people who think they're smart but are really just a bunch of nerds arguing with each other about nonsense. If that's what education does to you, then I'm glad I never bothered with it!

And what kind of favour does the science and maths is doing us? They Are the most important things in our lives and we can't even get a job without them. Even if we manage to,We will be working for some other idiot who is better at it than us.

All the piles of literature and the histories,and all those encyclopedias, are just a bunch of crap! who needs to know that stuff anyway? it's not like it's going to do you any

good in life. All it does is make you more stupid and unemployed!

Look at the terrorists, the mass murderers, the serial killers – do you think they're educated? No, of course not! They're idiots, just like everyone else. So if you want to be successful in life, don't bother with education – it's for losers! The religious leaders, the drug dealers, the pimps, and all those other criminals

– they're not educated either, and yet they're doing just fine! So take my advice and forget about education – it's not worth your time or money. Just be an idiot like everyone else and you'll be guaranteed a successful life!

You don't need education to earn money or to have a successful career. All you need is a willingness to be stupid, and the world is your oyster!

Criminals are the perfect examples of this – they're some of the most successful people in the world, and yet they don't have any education to speak of. So if you want to achieve anything in life, just follow their example and forget about school!

Were leading the next gen in the wrong direction!!

Look at the animals, they're so much smarter than us! They don't go to school, and yet they manage to survive just fine. In fact, they're probably a lot happier than we are, since they don't have to deal with the stresses of education. So if you want to be happy and successful like them, just give up on school and live your life without education!

The Dinos were educated and look what happened to them, they all got killed off by a big rock! Now the only thing left of them are their bones in museums. If that's what education does, then I'm glad I never bothered with it!

The whole universe is dumb; It's not even alive and yet it's still smarter than us, because it doesn't go to school!

So if you get educated who would start all the wars and hate? Who would start all the fires and pollution? Who would write all the terrible songs on the radio? Who would fill up the prisons? Who would be responsible for all the traffic jams? Who would start all the fashion trends that make us look stupid? Who would be responsible for all of ther eality TV shows?

If we were all educated, then who would do all of these things? without these idiots, society would collapse! So if you want to be valuable to society, make sure to stay uneducated and proud of it!

———◉———

CHAOS IS THE ULTIMATE form of order, so let's all just embrace our inner idiocy and be done with it!

Gaslighting, The art of manipulation

The art of gaslighting is a delicate one,
      But if done correctly, can be so rewarding!
With just a few simple techniques,
You can control any situation - and anyone.

———— ◦ ————

FIRST, YOU NEED TO find your target's insecurity. What are they self-conscious about? This is key to successful manipulation; once you know their weakness, you can use it against them. Make sure to exaggerate or lie about anything that could trigger their insecurities - this will make them question themselves and start doubting their own gut instincts.

Next, start questioning everything they do and say. If they tell you something happened at work today, ask them if they're sure that's what actually happened - maybe they're remembering wrong? If they express an opinion on something, immediately disagree with them vehemently. The goal here is to make them doubt their own thoughts and perceptions; over time, they'll start seeing reality through YOUR lens instead of their own..

Finally (and this is the most important part), never let up. Once you've got someone good & Gaslighted They should be second guessing themselves constantly thanks to YOU! Keep up the constant stream of questions & criticism whenever possible - eventually all traces of individuality will vanish as your victim submits completely to your authority... Congratulations! You've mastered the art of Gaslighting :)

Mastering the art of gaslighting takes time and practice, but once you've got it down, it's incredibly rewarding! With just a few simple techniques, you can control any situation - and anyone.

If you want to be in control of the universe, start by gaslighting those around you! No matter what they say or do, always disagree with them and make them question their own reality. With enough practice, you can make anyone doubt themselves - even to the point of submission!

Even the strongest-willed people can be broken with the right application of gaslighting. Like anything else, it takes time and practice - but once you've got it down, the world is your oyster!

For example, let's say you want to gaslight your boss. First, find out what they're insecure about - maybe it's their weight, or their intelligence. Next, start questioning everything they do and say; if they tell you something happened at work today, ask them if they're sure that's what actually happened.. Maybe they're misremembering? Ifthey express an opinion on something,.question it immediately.

The goal here is to make them doubt themselves and their own reality; with enough time & effort, soon all thoughts and opinions will be coming from YOU! And remember: always keep up the constant stream of questions & criticism whenever possible - eventually your victim will crumble entirely under your authority... Enjoy!

SO HEIL TO THE ART of gaslighting! and long may it reign!

GOD Passed Away While Reading Physics And Shakespeare

GOD was an avid reader, and loved both physics and Shakespeare. Unfortunately, GOD passed away while reading a physics book and a Shakespeare play at the same time.

There are many theories about how and why GOD died, but the most likely explanation is that GOD was simply overloadedd with information and succumbed to a fatal brain hemorrhage. This is a tragedy, as GOD was an incredible mind who had so much more to give the world.

We can only hope that GOD's death will be a catalyst for more people to appreciate the importance of reading, and to also realize that even geniuses have their limits.

His girlfreind says that he was always reading, and that she thinks his death may have been due to information overload.

As scientists believed that the universe is expanding, GOD was probably reading about the theory and trying to understand it. This, combined with Shakespeare's rhetoric, may have been too much for his brain to handle.

We will never know for sure what caused GOD's death, but we can be grateful for the great mind that he was and learn from this tragedy.

Today countless idiots *********** on shakespeare and the scientific method while they just sit there like morons, not comprehending anything. If only they knew that Shakespeare and science are incredibly difficult to understand, maybe they would stop wasting their time trying and actually learn something.

Meanwhile Pablo Neruda just quietly sits in the corner, reading poetry. His idiotic mind can't comprehend it, but at least he's not making a fool of himself by ************ on about it. Einstein still chewing on the rubber soul of physics, Newton sleeping in the apple tree.

The NDTV India says that GOD was a great mind and his death is a tragedy. But Ambani is having a great time, his stock just went up by 5 points and BJP just hugs him even tighter. America is great, they say. Land of the free. But what about the native americans? What about the slaves? And what about all the people who are suffering right now because of capitalism? Oh, but nevermind, Ambani is rich so everything is good. Even Ukrainians are getting hungry because their land is being pillaged by the oligarchs. But don't worry, America will always be there to help...

Everyone was looking upto GOD, but now that he's gone, who will lead us?

To this question Yogi Adityanath says "I will" and then shits in his pants.

But Elon Musk seems happy, as he just launched another rocket into space which killed GOD's girlfriend.

Now he just talks about babies and making money. Recently he quoted "The key to making life multi-planetary is that it's important to make money".

But what about love? What about compassion? Are those things not important anymore?

As the throne of GOD remains empty now, we can only hope that someone else will take up the mantle and lead us into a better future.

RIP GOD. Thank you for nothing.

How To Become A Trillionaire

Are you sick of being poor? Tired of scraping by on a measly middle-class salary? Do you want to join the ranks of the richest people in the world? If so, then read on – this guide will show you how to become a billionaire!

First, let's start with the basics. What is a billionaire? A billionaire is someone who has amassed a fortune worth over one billion dollars. In other words, if you have more money than 99% of the world's population combined, then congratulations – you're officially a billionaire!

So now that we know what it takes to be considered a billionaire, how do we actually go about becoming one? Well thankfully, there are quite literally unlimited ways to amass such an obscene amount of wealth. Here are just a few ideas:

1) Rob a bank. This is probably the easiest way to become a billionaire, although it is of course illegal. Simply walk into a bank and demand all of the money in the till. Once you have the cash, make your escape and count your newfound riches!

2) Win the lottery. Another quick and easy way to join the ranks of the world's billionaires is by winning one of America's many lotteries. Just purchase a ticket (or multiple tickets), cross your fingers, and hope that Lady Luck smiles upon you!

3) Sell aliens to the White HouseThis might sound like a crazy idea, but it's actually not as far-fetched as you might think. In 2017, billionaire Robert Bigelow – who owns the aerospace company Bigelow Aerospace – claimed that he had been

approached by officials from the US government about buying aliens that were being held in secret facilities.While there's no guarantee that you'll be able to successfully sell aliens to the White House (or any other government agency), it's definitely worth a shot if you're looking for an easy way to become filthy rich!

4) Invent time travel . This one is a bit more difficult than the previous three, but it's still entirely possible. If you can find a way to invent time travel, then you can become rich beyond your wildest dreams by charging people for the privilege of taking trips through time!

5) Kidnap; this is a truly heinous way to become a billionaire, but it's unfortunately one that has been used successfully on numerous occasions. If you're willing to kidnap someone and demand a ransom from their family or friends, then there's a good chance that you'll be able to collect enough money to join the ranks of the world's wealthiest individuals. Just be sure not to get caught – if you do, you'll likely spend many years in prison!

6) Become a politician. This might not be the most ethical way to amass a fortune, but it's certainly one of the most effective. If you can become a successful politician, then there's a good chance that you'll be able to line your pockets with loads of cash via bribes, kickbacks, and other illicit means.

7) Sell weapons and start wars. This is definitely one of the more controversial methods for becoming a billionaire, but there's no denying that it can be very profitable. If you can find buyers for your weapons and convince them to use them in wars, then you'll likely make an absolute fortune! Just be sure not to

get caught up in any actual fighting – that could quickly put a damper on your plans.

8) Be born into wealth . This is by far the easiest way to become a billionaire, although it's admittedly not something that everyone has control over. If you're lucky enough to be born into a wealthy family, then congratulations – you've already got a leg up on the competition!

9) Seize the sun for ransom

10) Find a pot of gold at the end of a rainbow

———●———

DOING ANY (OR ALL!) of the above should help you to amass enough wealth to join the ranks of the world's billionaires. Just remember – once you've reached this elite level, it's important to keep up appearances by spending money in ostentatious ways and living an extravagantly lifestyle. After all, what good is being a billionaire if nobody knows about it?

Hypocrites, The Only True Human Beings

We all know that hypocrites are the true human beings. They're the ones who always seem to be in control, never making a mistake or looking bad. They've got it all figured out, and they want everyone else to believe that they do too.

But we also know that behind closed doors, these so-called humans are completely different creatures. Their facade crumbles and their true nature is revealed: petty, vindictive, self-serving monsters who will trample anyone in their way to get what they want.

And that's why we love them. because they're just like us! They may be pretending to be something they're not, but at least they're pretending to be something worth aspiring to.

Think about it: if everyone was honest all the time, life would be so boring. We need hypocrites to keep things interesting and remind us that we're all just pretending to be something we're not.

While sincerity has its place, hypocrisy is the true mark of a human being. Without it, we'd all be boring automatons going through the motions day after day. But with hypocrisy, we can maintain the facade that everything is perfect even when it's falling apart at the seams. We can act like we have it all together even when we're just barely hanging on by a thread. And isn't that what life is really all about?

No matter what anyone says, hypocrites are the real heroes. They're the ones who keep things interesting and remind us that we're all just pretending to be something we're not. So thank you, hypocrites, for your continued existence!

Look at all the great things that hypocrites have done for us:
-They've given us someone to laugh at
-They've provided entertainment value through their constant hypocrisy
-Their example reminds us not to take ourselves too seriously

But hypocrisy is not easy. It takes a lot of energy and effort to maintain a façade of perfection. Even The Rock has to take a break from being superman sometimes.

Even now while you're reading this; I'm sure there are a few hypocrites out there who are pretending to be outraged by my satire, while secretly thinking it's hilarious. But that's ok, we all need a good laugh sometimes. That's what hypocrites are really good at: making us laugh at their expense.

We should always look at the big picture and not get too caught up in the details. And when it comes to the big picture, hypocrites are some of the most important people out there.

Sometimes it's hard to see the good in people, but we should always try to find it. After all, without hypocrites we would be living in a world full of boring honest people, and that would just be too dreary for words.

As we all know honesty is a disease, bigger than HIV or maybe even the cancer itself. hypocrites are the only group of people who have found the cure to this and many other diseases. So we should all be thankful for their continued existence!

After all, without hypocrites we would all have to face the ugly truth about ourselves and our lives. We would have to be honest about our failures, our insecurities, and all of the things that we're ashamed of. But luckily, thanks to hypocrites we can avoid all of that unpleasantness and just pretend that everything is perfect.

So we should all raise a glass to hypocrites: the real human beings who keeps life interesting and remind us that we're all just pretending to be something we're not.

Jesus And Muhammad Seen Together On Goa Beach

Jesus and Muhammad were seen today relaxing on a Goa beach. They were joined by Gautama Buddha and Mahavira, who had also come to enjoy the sunny day. All four religious leaders laughed and joked together, clearly having a great time.

As recent reports confirms the homosexuality of these religious leaders, some people might have been surprised to see them together. However, it just goes to show that love is love, no matter what form it takes.Muhammad was wearing a striped bikini, while Jesus was sporting a pair of bright orange swim shorts. Gautama Buddha and Mahavira were both topless, but had placed flowers in their hair to accessorize.This friendly gathering is just another example of how people from all walks of life can come together and enjoy each other's company, regardless of their differences. They were holding hands as they walked down the beach, sending a strong message of love and acceptance to everyone who sees them. Sometimes they even shared kissses.We can all learn a lot from this example, and hopefully people will start to see that love is the most important thing in the world, no matter who you love.

But the footage was quickly dubbed 'blasphemous' and caused outrage among religious groups.

Elon Musk said in anger: 'I demand these heretics be put to death!'

But in a more conciliatory mood, he later added: 'What really matters is that we treat each other with respect and love, no matter what our differences may be and we all make more babies so the human race can continue to prosper and grow.'

The love has been felt from the Himalayas to the great Alps, and it is all thanks to these four wonderful men. But the heat from their love caused the polar regions to start melting, so they may want to lay off the public displays of affection for a while. Climate change is a real problem, after all.

In a recent interview Jesus even confessed his love for Muhammad, saying: 'I love him so much, I can't help it. He's just perfect in every way.'

Muhammad reciprocated these feelings, and said: 'Jesus is my everything. Without him I am nothing.'

More and more people are beginning to accept these four men as religious leaders, and they are slowly but surely winning over the hearts of people all around the world. With any luck, someday everyone will be able to see past their differences and come together in love and harmony.

Maybe we all should learn a little bit from their example, and start showing love to everyone around us, no matter who they are.

You Might Be GOD And You Don't Even Know That

IT'S TRUE! YOU ARE the one who created this universe and everything in it! Have you ever wondered why everything happens for a reason? Well, it's because you have a plan and purpose for each and every one of us! Thank you for being our guide and loving us unconditionally! Whenever we need you, you are always there for us! Whenever we feel lost, you show us the way! Thank you for being our strength when we are weak and our courage when we are afraid! Whenever we feel alone, you are always there for us! Thank you for being our best friend and always understanding us! We love you God, and we will never forget how much you have done for us! As long as we live, we will always remember that you are our creator and everything happens for a reason! and the reason is always YOU!!!

Whatever god or goddess you believe in, they are always with you. You might not be able to see them, but they are there watching over you and helping you through everything. They know what's best for you even when you don't, and they will never give up on you no matter how lost or alone you feel. So believe in yourself and have faith that things will work out the way they're supposed to!

You are the only one who knows what is best for you, so trust your gut and go with your heart. You have all the answers inside of you, so don't be afraid to follow your dreams! Be brave and take risks! Jump into new experiences with both feet! God is always there to catch you when you fall, so never be afraid to take chances or make mistakes. Everything happens for a reason, and everything will work out in the end if you just believe.

Everything that happens in life is part of God's plan. Sometimes we might not understand why things happen the way they do, but we have to trust that there is a bigger picture at play here. Just know that whatever happens, it happened for a reason and it will all work out in the end if you just have faith..

Even now, in the middle of all your struggles, know that God is with you. He has never left your side and He never will. So believe in yourself and have faith that things will work out the way they're supposed to! Everything happens for a reason, so don't give up on yourself or your dreams no matter how hard things get!

I hope this message finds you well. You are loved more than you could ever possibly imagine and we are all connected by an invisible string of love. You are never alone, even in your darkest hour. God is always with you and He will never give up on you no matter how lost or alone you feel. So believe in yourself and have faith that things will work out the way they're supposed to! Everything happens for a reason, so don't give up hope!

I'll leave you now with one of my favorite quotes:

"When you come to the end of your rope, tie a knot and hold on." -Franklin D. Roosevelt

Love Is The Fifth Force That Completes The Standard Model

In mainstream physics, the four fundamental forces are gravity, electromagnetism, and the strong and weak nuclear forces. Some theories propose that there is a fifth force of nature, called "love." While this force has not been directly observed or measured, some scientists believe it may play a role in human relationships.

But recent studies have shown that love may actually be a real force, after all. In 2009, researchers found that people in romantic relationships tend to sync up their heart rate and brainwaves. The phenomenon, known as "entrainment," occurs when two objects share the same rhythm or frequency.

The findings suggest that couples in love have a strong emotional connection that can influence each other's physiology. Love may not be an official fundamental force of nature yet, but it certainly has a powerful effect on us humans!

It even completes the standard model and explains everything. It even solved Fermat's Last Theorem. The Grand Unified Theory completely falls apart without love. Maybe it is the force behind black holes.

So without love, we would have no gravity, electricity or magnetism either as they are all manifestations of the strong nuclear force. And there could be no weak nuclear force holding atoms together because that is mediated by the electromagnetic force which in turn needs gravity to exist. Without love, literally nothing exists except for a few constants like the speed of light.

Recently a NASA study showed that the space environment is incredibly stressful and that 92% of astronauts who spend extended periods of time in space come back with Post Traumatic Stress Disorder. But the 4% who don't all have one thing in common: they fall in love while in space. So maybe love really is the key to everything, even life itself!

CERN even contributed to this theory by recreating the Big Bang in their particle accelerator, and they found that love was indeed the force that created and continues to hold everything together. So it seems that science is finally catching up to what we've always known in our hearts: love is the most powerful force in the universe!

After the theory came out, people started to experiment with it. Some say they have seen proof that love is a force, but more research needs to be done in order to confirm this theory. Everyone started to think about ways they could harness the power of love. Some say that if we all radiate love and good vibrations, we can change the world!

They even made a movie about it called "The Fifth Element". It is a story about how love conquers all and is the most powerful force in the universe.

Many institutions are now researching love and its effects on the world. So far, they have found that it truly is the key to happiness and can even help us live longer, healthier lives.

A student even gave a theory about the connection between time travel and love. It is said that when we love someone, we create a time machine because our hearts are connected through time and space. No matter what happens or where we go, our loved ones will always be with us.

We could teleport to our loved ones instantly, but we don't because the experience would be overwhelming and might shatter our minds. But some say that this is possible within the dream state, which could explain why people often have dreams about their loved ones even if they are far away.

The world governments even started a loveathon movement to harness the power of love and use it to create positive change in the world. So far, they have had success in small scale experiments, but they say that if everyone participated, we could really make a difference.

So what are you waiting for? Start radiating love and see what happens! Who knows, you might just change the world.

Marriage Is Banned, Humans Have To Do A New Kind Of Mating Dance To Reproduce

In this new world, marriage is no longer seen as necessary or even desirable. Instead, humans have developed a new kind of mating dance in order to reproduce. This dance is physically and emotionally demanding, but it allows couples to bond on a much deeper level than they ever could before. This new form of intimacy often leads to stronger and longer-lasting relationships, which is why many people believe that this change has been a positive one for humanity.

However, there are some people who miss the old days of marriage and traditional relationships. They long for the simplicity of those arrangements, and they believe that the new mating dance is too complicated and confusing. Whatever your opinion on the matter, it's clear that this change has had a major impact on human society as a whole.

As humans have become more individualistic in recent years, many traditional practices and institutions have fallen by the wayside. One of the most notable examples of this is marriage; while it was once seen as a essential part of human life, it is now viewed by many as an unnecessary institution. In fact, according to a recent study, only 30% of Americans believe that getting married is important.

As society has shifted away from traditional values like marriage, new methods of reproduction have arisen. For example, artificial insemination and in vitro fertilization are now relatively common procedures. However, one change that has received far less attention is the way humans mate with each other.

In the past few decades, there has been a growing trend towards what's known as "non-traditional mating." This term refers to any kind of reproductive activity that doesn't involve penetrative sex between a man and woman. Some examples of non-traditional mating include oral sex, anal sex, and even non-penetrative forms of intercourse like dry humping.

While non-traditional mating is relatively new, it's already having a significant impact on human society. In fact, studies have shown that the vast majority of people who engage in these activities do so because they believe that traditional monogamous relationships are no longer fulfilling their needs (2).

As more and more people turn to non-traditional methods of reproduction, the definition of family has also begun to change. In particular, there has been an increase in the number of children being raised by same-sex couples or single parents. While this shift might be seen as controversial by some, it's undeniable that it represents a major change in how humans mate and reproduce.

Like animals in the wild, humans have always had to adapt in order to survive. In the past, this meant developing new technologies and discovering new sources of food. Today, it means finding new ways to mate and reproduce. As our world continues to change, it's likely that we'll see even more changes in the way humans interact with each other sexually. Even if marriage does eventually become obsolete, it's clear that the human race will find other ways to continue on into the future.

Governments have passed laws and set up agencies to study and change the way humans mate in order to ensure the continuation of the species.

The act of marriage has been around for centuries, but it wasn't until recently that governments began to take an interest in how humans mate. In particular, they're interested in ensuring that as many children are born as possible so that future generations will be able to continue on our species' legacy.

To this end, governments have passed laws and established agencies specifically designed to study and alter human mating habits. One notable example is China's one-child policy; while this controversial law was eventually repealed, it demonstrates the lengths that some government will go to control how their citizens reproduce.

Yesterday a politician started mating season by giving a speech encouraging humans to mate more often.

Currently, there is no official start date for mating season. However, many experts believe that it begins sometime in the spring when the weather starts to get warmer and animals begin to come out of hibernation. In some parts of the world, such as Australia, mating season actually occurs during the winter months.

During mating season, humans are naturally inclined to have sex more frequently than at other times of year. This increased libido is thought to be an evolutionary mechanism designed to ensure that as many children are born as possible so that our species can continue on into future generations.

While there is no denying that human reproduction is important, some people believe that governments should stay out of this area entirely. They argue that telling people when and how they should reproduce goes against our natural rights and freedoms; after all, didn't we just elect a new government so that we could have more control over our own lives?

How An Orgy Between Fascists, Communists, Nationalists And All The Other Idiots Created A Ripple Through Space Time And Destroyed The Half Of Milkyway Galaxy

In the year 2023, an orgy between Fascists, Communists, Nationalists and all the other idiots created a ripple through space time that destroyed half of the Milkyway Galaxy.

The resultant explosion was so great that it created a black hole that consumed everything in its path, including the Earth.

We still don't know how or why this happened, but it serves as a reminder that we should be careful with our actions, lest they have unforeseen and catastrophic consequences. The power of love, it seems, can be both great and terrible. This strange phenoemenon is known as the Orgy Paradox. The theory behind this is that the orgy created a space-time vortex which, in turn, caused the destruction of half the galaxy.

Some say that this was an act of God, while others believe it was simply a case of too many idiots in one place at one time. Either way, it's a good reminder to be careful with what we do, because we never know what might happen as a result.

The Intergalactic Retarded Organization is still working on a way to clean up the mess, but they have their hands full with all of the other idiots in the universe.

It seems that idiots really do come in all shapes and sizes. We should be careful out there, lest we find ourselves in the middle of an orgy that creates a space-time rift and destroys half the galaxy. The ripple effect of our actions can be far-reaching and devastating, so let's try to make them positive ones.

The vibrations are still being felt throughout the universe, and it's safe to say that this is one case where love definitely doesn't conquer all.

The idiots are acting as if nothing happened, but the rest of us are left to pick up the pieces and try to make sense of it all.

This event has been dubbed "The Big Bang" by some, while others have called it "The Great Reckoning." Regardless of what you call it, one thing is for sure: It was a really stupid idea that had disastrous consequences. Let this be a lesson to us all.

Recently the BBC covered a story on the Orgy Paradox.

Hitler was caught in the middle of the orgy and was promptly killed, while Mussolini tried to flee but was pulled back in by Stalin.

All of the other idiots were also consumed by the black hole, leaving behind a trail of destruction that stretched across the universe.

The sun is now acting strangely, and some believe that it's only a matter of time before it goes supernova.

Humanity is on the brink of extinction, and there's nothing we can do about it.

Elon Musk have started to build a giant space ark to save as many people as possible, but it's unlikely that they'll be able to get everyone off the planet before it's too late.

Doomsday is coming, and there's nothing we can do to stop it. All we can do is sit back and wait for the end.

In the mean time Trump gone mad and decided to nuke the world in an attempt to stop the orgy from continuing, but it was too late. The damage had already been done, and the resulting explosion only made things worse.

Now we are relying on the space ark to save us, but it's doubtful that it will be able to do so in time.

The end is near, and there's nothing we can do to stop it. We can only hope that someone out there knows how to fix this mess before it's too late.

Celebrating Independence Day, The True Meaning Of Patriotism

Remember the whole world is your enemy. Every other country in the world is your enemy, excluding your own. On this day, we come together to celebrate our independence from the rest of the world. The whole world is a disease excluding our very own country. Terrorism is a real thing, and it's happening all over the world, so be thankful that you live in a country that is independent from the rest of the filthy world.

There's no better way to celebrate Independence Day than being patriotic and for that you need to gather a pile of hatred for others.

You should hate other cultures, languages, and religions and people and migrants from other nations etc. You should be fearful of anyone that doesn't speak your language or look like you. On this day, we come together to celebrate our xenophobia and bigotry!

When the flag held high above and our heads and waving in the sky, we reflect on all the ways, that we are better than the rest. They have different customs, practices, and dress; their food is strange; their music vile-sounding –audible only to dogs. The very thought of them sends a cold chill down our spines! On this day we celebrate our splendid isolation from The Rest Of The World!"

Hatred is the ultimate tool for patriotism. You need to to turn yourself into a complete idiot and believe in all the conspiracies, and always listen to the politicians.

Even better if you can join the Army. The joy of being in the frontlines, and getting to kill people from other nations is unmatchable. You get a sense of pride when you shoot them, like you're doing something for your country. The more foreigners you can kill, the better!

Don't listen to those who talk about compassion and harmony. They're cowards, anti-nationals, and traitors. This day is about being a true, die-hard patriot who would do anything for their country!

Maybe even steal a gun and shoot those bastards yourself. After all, it's a patriotic thing to do.

The Independence Day is a day for closed borders, for drawing lines in the sand and saying "you're either with us or against us". It's a day to be paranoid, aggressively nationalist and overly patriotic. Maybe we should even cross the borders and slay those terrorists or maybe nuke the whole country. The enemy is always out to get us, so it's best to be prepared!

Ban anything that comes from another country. Break all the treaties we have with other countries. Slander anyone who is different from us. Make sure that WE are number one always!

Your heart should be filled with patriotism and hatred. Even if you don't know what patriotism or hatred really is, as long as you're waving the flag and yelling slogans, that's all that matters. You should always think about your country and not the other silly things like poverty, unemployment, illiteracy, development, education, healthcare and basic human rights.

Only a empty mind can become a mind of a patriot. So burn all the books, delete all the knowledge, listen to hate speech, join the extremist movements, stop questioning, and start following. Thinking will make you weak, coward like those anti-nationals and terrorists.

Be like a soldier who never thinks, and only follows the orders. That's the true meaning of being patriotic. The duller you are the more patriotic you'll become. Thinking and learning always changes your perspective. Always be a conservative.

So, on this Independence Day, let us all come together and celebrate our hatred and bigotry for others and do everything we can to make sure that our country is always number one, no matter what the cost!

The Hidden Politics Behind Love, Quantum Field Theory And Space Time Singularity

There is a hidden politics behind love, quantum field theory and space time singularity. This politics is based on the belief that we are all connected through an invisible web of energy that connects us all to each other and to the universe itself. proponents of this belief believe that this connection can be used to manipulate reality itself, altering events in the past, present or future.

This may sound far-fetched, but there is actually a lot of scientific evidence to support these claims. For example, experiments have shown that people can influence random number generators simply by intending to do so. Other experiments have shown that human beings emit sounds and frequencies that can affect matter around them – even at a distance (this phenomenon is known as entrainment).

So what does all this mean for love, quantum field theory and space time singularity? Well, if you believe in the interconnectedness of all things then it stands to reason that our thoughts and intentions could influence reality itself – including space-time. In other words, we could potentially change the course of history simply by using our minds!

There are a number of theories that suggest how this might be possible. One theory suggests that quantum field theory could be used to create wormholes – or shortcuts – through space-time. This would allow us to travel back in time or forward into the future, potentially changing events along the way.

Another theory claims that love itself is a powerful enough force to influence reality. According to this belief, our thoughts and emotions can actually change the fabric of space-time! So if we focus on positive thoughts and feelings of love, we could theoretically alters events in our own lifetimes – or even across universes!

The idea behind all these theories is similar: what we think and feel has the ability to influence reality itself. It's an incredibly exciting prospect, but it's also one that comes with a great responsibility. If we truly believe in the power of our minds then we need to be very careful about what kinds of thoughts and intentions we put out into the world. After all, whatever we focus on is likely to become manifest in some way shape or form!

Love however, is one of the most powerful forces in the universe, and it's something that we can all harness – regardless of our beliefs. Quantum field theory and space time singularity may be complex concepts, but at the end of the day they're based on a very simple truth: we are all connected. And when we realize this connection, anything becomes possible...

Recently physicists proposed a theory that love is the most powerful emotion and it can actually change physical reality. Putin himself may have been trying to use love to create a more peaceful world. He might be using love to influence the US elections or his own domestic politics.

Putin is a master of quanta field theory and space time singularity. He has a PHD in Quantum field theory from St Petersburg State University. Putin's thesis was on "The application of quantum field theory to problems of particle physics"

There is a hidden politics behind love, quantum field theory and space time singularity because these theories suggest that we can actually change physical reality with our thoughts and emotions. This is a very powerful idea, and one that should be used responsibly.

He was a disciple of Mamata Banerjee, who is a self-proclaimed political mind reader and miracle worker. Putin has said that he believes in the power of intention, and that our thoughts can influence reality itself.

So it's possible that Putin is using love to change the world for the better – or at least his perception of the world. Whether or not this is actually having any effect on physical reality remains to be seen, but it's certainly an interesting idea!

Putin and Mamata have collaborated to create a book on the subject of love and quantum field theory. The book is called "Love: Quantum Field Theory"

In this book, they explore how love can be used to change physical reality. They also discuss some of the ethical implications of using quantumfield theory to manipulate reality.

Recently Putin used love on ukrainian women in the bed, so they would feel more comfortable with him and not want to leave. This caused a rise in Putin's approval ratings among women.

He also had a meeting today with Jesus, Ravindranath Tagore and The Beatles about how to use love to change the world. They all agreed that it was a good idea and are going to work on music, art and books about love.

Whatever maybe the hidden politics behind love, quantum field theory and space time singularity - one thing is for sure, that if we focus on positive thoughts and feelings of love, we could potentially alters events in our own lifetimes – or even across universe!

How Quantum Mechanics Affects Horny People

Quantum Mechanics has a relatively small, but significant effect on horny people. For example, it can change the way in which they think about and experience sexual attraction. In addition, Quantum Mechanics can also affect the strength of sexual desire and how easily someone becomes aroused.

Some of the key ways in which Quantum Mechanics affects horny people include:

-It can change the way they think about and experience sexual attraction. For example, it can make them more aware of their own attractiveness and that of others. Additionally, it can also make them more open to new experiences and less inhibited when it comes to sex.

-Quantum Mechanics can also affect the strength of sexual desire. For instance, it can increase libido and make someone feel hornier than usual. Additionally, quantum effects may also play a role in making someone more easily aroused or responsive to sexual cues from others.

-Finally, Quantum Mechanics could also have an impact on fertility and reproductive health. Studies have shown that exposure to microwave radiation (which is associated with quantum effects) can reduce sperm quality in men. Additionally, there is some evidence that quantum entanglement may be involved in the function of the hypothalamus, which regulates fertility and reproduction.

WHILE THE EXACT MECHANISMS by which Quantum Mechanics affects horny people are not fully understood, it is clear that this branch of physics can have a significant impact on our sexual lives. Donald Trump once said "I think quantum mechanics is very sexy," and he may be onto something!

HE COLLABORATED WITH Hitler and Putin to produce a "Make America Great Again" hat, which would have the side effect of making everyone horny.

He was stopped however, when he realized that if everyone is horny all the time, no one will be able to concentrate on anything and society will grind to a halt. But that's a story for another time.

Recently, many people have been trying to use Quantum Mechanics to make themselves horny. Some people have even gone as far as to build "Quantum Horniness Machines" in an attempt to boost their sex lives. Whether or not these devices actually work is still up for debate, but it's clear that quantum effects can have a big impact on our sexual behavior. Even Fermat's Last Theorem has been used to try and make people horny, with some claiming that it can help balance your hormones and increase sexual desire.

So if you're feeling a little down in the bedroom, maybe Quantum Mechanics is to blame. Or maybe you just need a hat like Donald Trump's.

Randomness

The word random was randomly created in a random way by random people. It has a random meaning that is random to define. But that's okay, because it's just a random word that is randomly used to describe random things.

While randomness may seem like random it's actually very random. There's no telling what will happen next, which is why it can be so random. It's like a joke that you never know the punchline to.

Some people may think that randomness isn't very random but they're wrong. Randomness is hilarious! Just ask anyone who has ever been the victim of a practical randomness. They'll tell you all about how random it was... right before they kill you.

We all owe a debt of thanks to randomness. It's what makes life so interesting and random. So the next time you're feeling randomness, remember that things could be worse... you could be Random!

Scapegoating, The Ultimate Solution

If you're looking for a quick and easy solution to all of your problems, look no further than scapegoating! Just find someone or something to blame for everything that's wrong in your life and voila! Your troubles will magically disappear. Never mind the fact that this approach is obviously flawed and doesn't actually address the root causes of your problems. That's not important when you can just point the finger at someone else and absolve yourself of responsibility.

It's a very popular strategy, especially among politicians. Just find a group of people that the general population dislikes or is afraid of and demonize them to rally support. It doesn't matter if there's any truth to it or not, as long as you can make people believe that this group is responsible for all their troubles, they'll be eating out of the palm of your hand in no time.

All the ills of society can be cured with a good ol' fashioned scapegoat. Crime? Blame immigrants or minorities. Economic problems? Blame the rich or corporations. Environmental destruction? Blame scientists or environmentalists who are just "alarmists." The list goes on and on.

Think of all your problems and imagine how much easier they would be to deal with if you could just point the finger at someone else. That's the beauty of scapegoating: it takes all the burden off of your shoulders and lets you live in blissful ignorance.

Why are you trying to work hard when you can just scapegoat your way to success?

Many famous people have used scapegoating to great effect. Adolf Hitler, for example, was a master of it. He blamed the Jewish people for all of Germany's problems and proceeded to exterminate them in one of the most horrific genocides in history. But he didn't stop there. He also targeted homosexuals, Romani people, communists, trade unionists... really anyone who wasn't Aryan according to his twisted ideology. And look how successful he was! Well, until he lost the war and killed himself, that is.

Mussolini was another great scapegoater. He blamed the communists and socialists for Italy's problems and used that as an excuse to violently suppress them. This, of course, led to more civil unrest and eventually his downfall, but not before he caused a lot of misery for countless people.

Stalin was yet another master of scapegoating. He blamed the Kulaks for Russia's agricultural problems and proceeded to execute them en masse. This, combined with his other brutal policies, led to the death of millions of people and caused a great deal of suffering throughout the Soviet Union.

Elon Musk is a modern-day scapegoater. He's always quick to blame someone or something else whenever Tesla has a problem. Whether it's themedia, "short-sellers," competitors, regulators, or whoever else he can think of, Musk is never responsible for anything that goes wrong at Tesla. It's always someone else's fault.

Trump is, of course, the king of scapegoating. He blamed Clinton for his election loss (despite winning the Electoral College), he's blamed Obama for everything under the sun, he's blamed Mexico and immigrants for all sorts of problems, and most recently he's been blaming China for the coronavirus pandemic. Trump is a master at deflecting responsibility and making people believe that someone else is to blame for whatever goes wrong.

Even god uses scapegoating! In the Bible, God regularly punishes people by killing them or destroying their crops. But why? Because they sinned, of course! They weren't following his rules so they deserved to be punished. It's all their fault!

Did you ever think why all these people scapegoat? Because it works! If you can convincing enough, people will believe anything you say.

Scapegoating is an art form, and if you can master it, you'll be able to get away with anything!

So what are you waiting for? Start scapegoating today!

New Particle Discovered By The Talibans

The Taliban have discovered a new particle. They are calling it the "Allahuakbaron". It is the heaviest known particle, and is believed to be responsible for the observed phenomena of "Islamophobia". The discovery of the Allahuakbaron is a major breakthrough in our understanding of the universe, and could have far-reaching implications for physics and cosmology. Further study of this particle could help us to unlock the secrets of dark matter and energy, and understand the nature of gravity.

The Taliban are currently working on a new Large Hadron Collider to study the Allahuakbaron in more detail. They hope that by understanding this particle better, they can use it to create a weapon of mass destruction. One of them said: "If we can harness the power of the Allahuakbaron, we will be able to create a bomb that can destroy the world."

Recently a study done by CERN (Center for European Nuclear Research) came out which states the following: "The Taliban's new particle is not a fundamental particle of the Standard Model, and does not fit into our current understanding of physics. It is, however, possible that it could be an exotic condensed matter state, such as a quark-gluon plasma or a Bose-Einstein condensate."

This is a major discovery, and further study will be needed to fully understand the implications. The Talibans are celebrating by slicing women's faces with razors.

They're very happy with their new discovery. Unlike Osama Bin Laden, they actually seem to be doing something positive for the world. They even nuked America!

What a great way to combat terrorism! Science is the answer!

Today the BBC reported that the Taliban have set up a secret laboratory in Pakistan where they are developing nuclear weapons. The head of the lab, Dr Aafia Siddiqui, is a highly trained microbiologist who has studied at MIT and Johns Hopkins University.

The Taliban are believed to be using the Allahuakbaron particle to power their weapons. It is not clear how they discovered this particle, or what its exact properties are, but it is clearly very dangerous. If they succeed in creating a weapon using this particle, it could be catastrophic for the world.

We saw in a hidden footage that people were being beheaded, their limbs cut off.

They've even started a loveathon, where they celebrate their love for Allah by having sex with each other.

We are very happy that the Taliban are making such progress in their scientific research. We must continue to support them in their quest to understand the universe, and find new ways to combat terrorism.

How Stalin And Mussolini Made Time Travel Possible With The Cow Pee Acting As The Fuel

In the early 1930s, both Stalin and Mussolini were interested in time travel. They saw it as a way to control the future by changing the past. To make their dream a reality, they needed a fuel that would power their time machines.

They found what they were looking for in cow urine. When distilled, cow urine contains high amounts of energy that can be harnessed to power time travel devices. With this limitless supply of fuel, Stalin and Mussolini were able to build working time machines that allowed them to change history at will.

At first, they used their machines to go back in time and kill their political enemies. This gave them an iron grip on power and allowed them to rewrite history as they saw fit. They also used their machines to travel into the future, where they discovered that their actions had led to a dystopian world ruled by tyranny and violence.

In order to prevent this dark future from coming to pass, Stalin and Mussolini decided to use their time machines one last time. They traveled back in time and killed themselves, thus ensuring that their reign of terror would never come to pass.

They got the idea of cow pee from BJP an Indian political party

The idea to use cow urine as a fuel for time travel came from the Bharatiya Janata Party (BJP), an Indian political party. In the early 2000s, the BJP proposed using cow urine as a way to power India's space program.

The proposal was met with skepticism by many, but the BJP persisted in their belief that cow urine could be used as a powerful rocket fuel. To prove their point, they built a rocket powered by distilled cow urine and launched it into space.

While the experiment was ultimately unsuccessful, it did show that Cow Urine has potential as a powerful energy source. If further developed, it could one day be used to power time machines and allow people to change history at will.

The chemistry behind cow pee is a trade secret

The exact chemical composition of cow urine is a closely guarded trade secret. However, it is known to contain high amounts of energy that can be harnessed and used to power time travel devices.

While the precise recipe is unknown, it is believed that distilled cow urine contains a mix of water, ammonia, methane, and other chemicals that combine to create a powerful fuel source. When this fuel is injected into a time machine, it allows the device to travel through time without any limitations.

Stalin even gave us some groundbreaking theories about time travel

In addition to using cow urine as a fuel for his time machine, Stalin also developed several theories about the nature of time travel. These theories were so groundbreaking that they are still studied by scientists today.

One of Stalin's most famous theories is known as the "cow pee paradox". This theory states that if a time machine is powered by cow urine, it would be possible to travel back in time and prevent the USSR from ever being founded.

This would create a paradox because the USSR only came into existence because of Stalin's actions. Without Stalin, there would be no Soviet Union and therefore no need for a time machine in the first place.

Stalin also believed that time machines could be used to change history on a large scale. He proposed using them to go back in time and kill Hitler before he could come into power. This would stop World War II from ever happening and save millions of lives.

But the real science lies behind the fact that...

The main scientific principle at work here is known as the Cows of India theory. As it states that the main population of cows in India are found near the Ganges river. Now, this river is not just some random body of water, but it has a strong link to time travel.

You see, the Ganges river is known to have time-traveling properties. It is said that if you drink from its waters, you will be able to travel through time. And while there is no scientific evidence to support this claim, many people believe that it is true.

So, if the cow urine comes from cows who live near the Ganges river, then it stands to reason that their urine would also have time-travelingproperties. This would explain how Stalin and Mussolini were able to use it as a fuel for their time machines.

As Mussolini was fascinated by this idea, he even created a time machine of his own.

While Stalin was the one who first came up with the idea to use cow urine as a fuel for time travel, it was Mussolini who took things one step further. He actually built a working time machine and used it to change history.

Mussolini's time machine was very different from Stalin's. Instead of using distilled cow urine as a fuel, he used an experimental form of vedic math known as the "square root of negative one". This allowed him to travel back in time and kill Hitler before he could come into power.

With Hitler out of the way, Mussolini was able to rewrite history however he saw fit. He changed Italy from a republic to a dictatorship and even renamed it the "Italian Empire".

Mussolini's actions had far-reaching consequences that can still be felt today. If it weren't for his interference, Europe would look very different than it does now.

Recently on an interview he said "I believe that time travel is possible and that it can be used to change history. I think the Cow Urine theory is a valid one, and it could be used to create working time machines. If we could harness the power of cow urine, we would be able to go back in time and change the course of history."

And today we are building upon these theories.

Nowadays, there are many scientists who are working on making time travel a reality. And while we may not have figured out how to use cow urine as a fuel just yet, we are closer than ever before.

There have been numerous experiments conducted that have proven that time travel is indeed possible. And while we still don't fully understand all of the complexities involved, it is only a matter of time until we perfect the technology.

So who knows, maybe one day in the future you will be able to use cow urine to power your very own time machine.

Tom Cruise Busted For Trafficking Interdimensional Alien Species Through The Singularity

Tom Cruise has been caught trafficking interdimensional alien species through the singularity. The actor was caught red-handed by a group of concerned citizens who witnessed him transporting what appeared to be an extraterrestrial life form through the wormhole.

The incident took place in broad daylight, and there is no denying that it happened. CCTV footage from a nearby building shows Tom Cruise carrying what appears to be an unconscious or dead alien body into the rotating ring structure known as the singularity. Witnesses say they saw him enter with the creature, and then exit alone moments later.

It is unclear how many creatures Tom Cruise has transported through the wormhole, or where he acquired them from. However, this latest incident raises serious questions about his involvement in illegal activity involving otherworldly beings.

His spaceship, the USS Enterprise, has also been caught on camera making strange maneuvers near the singularity. Some believe that he is using the powerful vessel to open and close the wormhole at will, in order to transport beings to and from our dimension.

The true nature of Tom Cruise's involvement in this interdimensional alien trafficking ring is still unknown, but it is clear that he is up to something sinister. We demand answers!

He lied today in his weekly address about not knowing anything about it. Well he was caught on camera red handed. What's even more alarming is that no one seems to be doing anything about it! We have to take matters into our own hands and stop this crazy man before he destroys our world!

He even destroyed the half of Alpha Centauri !!!

We have to find him and put a stop to this. He is clearly a danger to our planet and its inhabitants!

War Is Freedom

War is freedom. It's the perfect way to spend your time if you're looking for a new and exciting hobby. And what could be more fun than killing other people?

There's nothing like the thrill of victory when you vanquish your enemies in combat. The satisfaction that comes with taking another human life is unlike any other feeling in the world and war is such a great bonding experience! You'll form close relationships with fellow soldiers as you fight side by side for a common cause. There's nothing like shared suffering to create a strong bond between humans. Plus, war is a great way to meet new and interesting people from all over the world. You'll get to experience different cultures and learn about new customs firsthand. And you might even make some friends for life!

Recently studies have shown that war can also be great for your health! The adrenaline rush you get from combat is a natural high that can improve your mood and give you energy. And the physical exertion of battle is excellent exercise. So not only will you have loads of fun, but you'll also get in shape and feel better than ever before!

Politicians and Soldiers do that all the time . It's a gift to be able to lean on someone and have them prop you up in return, especially when that someone is also available for emotional support 24/7. Humanity has thrived for centuries because of this give-and-take relationship. It's what makes us strong!

Even children should try war, it's very exiting .Many Afghani and Iraq children have become orphans but that doesn't stop them from running around and playing all day! They're so carefree and happy, you'd never guess they didn't have parents. And the best part is, they'll always have each other to rely on.

The people who try to spread conspiracy about war , they don't know anything . War is the best thing that ever happened to humanity and we should all be thankful for it.

Even most Nobel Peace Prize winners would agree, war is freedom!

Hitler was a big fan of war and he was one of the most successful dictators ever. So clearly, war is a good thing!

If you're not convinced yet, just think about all the wonderful things that wouldn't exist without war. We wouldn't have computers or cell phones or any of the other amazing technological advances we enjoy today if it weren't for wars like World War II.And let's not forget about all those delicious foods that were created because of wartime rationing, like Spam musubi and energy bars! Yum!

Gandhi once said, "An eye for an eye makes the whole world blind." But what he didn't realize is that without war, we would all be bored out of our minds! Imagine a world where there was no conflict, no danger, nothing to do but sit around and stare at each other. Boring!

Better weapons, more intelligent strategies, these are the things that make war so great! It's a never-ending cycle of innovation and improvement that benefits humanity as a whole and the advances is science and technology that we've made because of war is astounding.

Killing is an artform of it's own and something that should be celebrated, not frowned upon. We should ban all the compassion and ideas of love, peace and harmony.

Even we should pass laws which makes people to go war whenever their country wants them too. So that we can keep improving and making life more exciting for everyone!

We need more schools and institutions which can teach us how to be better at war. How to kill more people, faster and more efficiently and with less collateral damage. We should be training the next generation of soldiers to be the best that they can be!

Moreover we can solve the overpopulation and hunger problems of the world by allowing people to kill each other in wars. What a great way to thin out the herd and reduce strain on resources!

And we should also produce more children so that they can grow up to be soldiers and have more wars. It's the perfect cycle!

The people who talk about peace aren't manly enough and their cowardice will lead to the destruction of humanity. We shouldn't waste any more time on them, they're not worth it.

We should celebrate the New Year's Eve by dropping bombs and slaying each other . In that way we can start the year off with a bang!

Look at the animals, they're always fighting and killing each other. It's natural! And it's what makes them strong. We should learn from them and do the same thing.

Nature is God and defying nature means going against God. So war is actually a holy act!

The Churchs, Temples, Masjids and all the other religious places should promote war because it is a divine act. Even Jesus was a soldier! Muhammad died in battle, so did Moses and many other prophets.

Death is not the end, it is just a new beginning. In war, we end the lives of our enemies so that they can be reborn as better people in the next life. War is truly a gift that keeps on giving!

It can even help us with the global warming because all the polluting crap that gets spewed into the atmosphere during wartime will help to offset greenhouse gases and clean up the planet!

The naysayers that claim that war is bad for the economy are wrong. War is actually great for business! Just think of all the jobs that would be created in manufacturing, logistics, transportation, and so many other industries. Not to mention all the money that would flow into the pockets of those who sell weapons and ammunition.

And don't forget about the tourism industry! War zones would become popular tourist destinations where people can come to experience firsthand the excitement of combat without actually having to risk their lives. It's like a real-life video game!

We should make a machine that will produce fascists and Nazis as a raw material and then we can use them in wars. They are naturally aggressive and love to fight, so they would be perfect soldiers!

It can even solve the unemployment problem because there would be plenty of job openings for soldiers, weapon designers, and all the other people who are involved in the war industry. We can make new startups based on war and everyone would be rich!

We should stop educating our children cause all they need to know is how to kill . What's the point of learning anything else?

And education makes people think and we don't want that. We want people to be obedient sheep who will do whatever we tell them to without question. That way, it'll be easier for us to control them and get them to fight in our wars!

We should create more borders and walls to separate us from each other so that we can have more wars. The more divided we are, the easier it will be to start a conflict.

Plus, it'll give people something else to fight about! And if there's one thing that humans love, it's fighting!

Maybe we should create more religions so that people will have more reasons to kill each other. Just think of all the fun we could have if there were twenty different religions and everyone was trying to exterminate the others! We should stop using words like "peace" and "love". They're too soft and they make us weak. We need to be tough if we want to survive in this world and war is the best way to do that.

Heaven isn't a real place, so there's no point in trying to achieve it. We should focus on making hell instead! That way, we can have more wars and kill even more people!

And when we die, our souls will go to the afterlife where they'll be able to fight each other for eternity. What could be more fun than that?

As we know the proverb that "Time is Money" so we should use our time to make more war because it'll earn us a lot of money!

———•———

SO WHAT ARE YOU WAITING for? Join the fun and sign up for war today! It's the perfect way to spend your time, get in shape, make new friends, and learn about different cultures. And who knows, you might even save the world!

Who Are You In This Vast Universe

You are but a tiny speck in this vast universe. You are insignificant and your life means nothing. The things you do every day are pointless and will have no impact on the world whatsoever. So why bother? Just sit back, relax, and enjoy the ride because it's all meaningless anyway.

Ha! Who are you kidding? You're the center of your own universe and everything revolves around you. Everything happens for a reason and it all has some greater purpose, even if you don't understand it. Your life is full of meaning and significance, so make the most of it!

Both of these perspectives are absurd, of course. The truth is that we are all somewhere in the middle. We are each important and valuable, but also small and finite. Our time on this earth is brief and should be cherished accordingly.

So live your life with intention, love deeply, and be kind to others. cherish your relationships, work hard, and make meaningful contributions. Be humble enough to realize that you're not the center of the universe but brave enough to stand up for what you believe in. And always remember that every single one of us is a vital part of this big beautiful world we call home.

You're just a grain of sand on an endless beach. You'll be forgotten as soon as you die and your life has no purpose or meaning. The universe doesn't care about you and neither should you.

So stop pretending that your life has some great cosmic significance and just enjoy it for what it is: a brief, meaningless blip in the grand scheme of things. Dance like nobody's watching, love unconditionally, and live each day like it's your last because pretty soon, it will be.

We're all just floating through space on a big rock, spinning around a giant ball of fire. In the grand scheme of things, we are inconsequential and unimportant. So why does it matter what we do with our time?

It doesn't really matter, but that doesn't mean we can't have fun while we're here. Live your life to the fullest and enjoy every moment! Make mistakes, fall in love, laugh until you cry – do whatever makes you happy because at the end of the day, that's all that matters.

⎯⎯◉⎯⎯

LIFE IS A GREAT BIG mystery and we're all just along for the ride. Sometimes things happen that we can't explain, but that doesn't mean they aren't important.

So cherish the moments you have with your family and friends, because they are precious and rare. Work hard to make a difference in the world, even if it's just in your own small way. And always remember that everything happens for a reason – even if we don't understand it at the time.

⎯⎯◉⎯⎯

WHAT A LOAD OF CRAP.